MW00962431

I Am Generous!

by David Parker
Illustrated by Cristina Ong

SCHOLASTIC INC.
New York Toronto London Auckland Sydney
Mexico City New Delhi Hong Kong Buenos Aires

To my younger brother Tommy — who gives his time, his heart,
and his humor to everyone, and to Uncle Mike and Aunt Ida —
who taught me there is always room for one more at the table.
— D.P.

To Xylia, second only to the Most Generous,
and to Christel for the heart.
— C.O.

ISBN 0-439-62813-X

Text copyright © 2004 by David Parker
Illustrations copyright © 2004 by Cristina Ong
All rights reserved. Published by Scholastic Inc.
SCHOLASTIC, THE BEST ME I CAN BE™ Readers, and associated logos are trademarks
and/or registered trademarks of Scholastic Inc.

12   6 7 8 9/0

Printed in the U.S.A.
First printing, March 2004

Guess how you would feel—
if you shared your favorite book with a friend.

Guess how you would feel—
if you smiled at someone who looked sad.

Guess how you would feel—
if you read a story to your sister or brother.

Guess how you would feel—
if you cheered up an older person.

Guess how you would feel—
if you said something nice to the new kid in school.

Guess how you would feel—
if you set the table before anybody asked you.

Guess how you would feel—
if you saved pennies for children who were hungry.

Guess how you would feel—if you made a card
for a sick friend.

Guess how you would feel—if you did a favor for someone and didn't tell that it was you.

You would feel GOOD—

because you are being GENEROUS!

Being generous means you give to others because you want to.

That makes you feel really good inside.

How will you be generous today?